THE CURSE OF CLIFTON.

CHAPTER I.

THE MOUNTAIN HUT.

Upon a glorious morning in the midsummer of 18—, two equestrian travellers spurred their horses up the ascent of the Eagle's Flight, the loftiest and most perilous pass of the Alleghanies.

Though the sun was near the meridian, and all the sky above was "darkly, deeply, beautifully blue," and perfectly clear, yet all the earth beneath was covered by a thick, low-lying fog.

On reaching the highest point of the pass, both travellers drew rein and paused, looking—north, south, east, west—over the ocean of vapour rolling from horizon to horizon below them! And while they so pause, let us catch that nearly vertical ray of the sun that falls upon them, lighting up the group like fire above the fog, and daguerreotype them as they stand.

Both are young men of about the same age, probably twenty-five; both are well mounted upon fine bay horses; and both wear the undress uniform of the —— regiment of Cavalry—and here all resemblance between them ceases.

He on the right hand, who holds in his horse's head with so tight a rein, causing the gallant steed to arch his beautiful neck so gracefully, while he lets fly a falcon-glance around the shrouded horizon, is Archer Clifton of Clifton, now holding the rank of Captain in the —— regiment of Cavalry. His form is of middle size, strongly built, yet elegantly proportioned; his complexion is dark and bronzed as by exposure; his features are Roman; his hair and whiskers, trimly cut, are of the darkest chestnut, with what painters

B

call *cool* lights; which is to say, that there is no warmth of colouring even where the sun lights. Indeed, there is no warmth about the looks of the whole man. His eyes are singularly beautiful and brilliant, combining all those dark, shifting, scintillating, prismatic hues that would drive an artist mad for want of colours to portray, or an author to despair for lack of words to describe. He wears the dark blue uniform of his regiment, and manages his noble charger with the ease and grace only to be found in the accomplished cavalry officer.

He upon the left hand, who, with languid air and loosened rein, inclines his body forward, permitting his graceful horse to droop his head and scent the earth, as in quest of herbage, is Francis Fairfax, of Green Plains, a lieutenant in the company under the command of Captain Clifton. He is of about the same height as Clifton, but his figure is slender almost to fragility. His features are delicate and piquant. His complexion is fair and transparent. His hair is also very fair, and waves off from a forehead so snowy, round, and smooth, as to seem child-like, especially with those clear blue eyes, that now brood roguishly under their golden lashes, as in profound quest of mischief, and now light up and sparkle with fun and frolic. He *mis*-manages his spoiled pet of a steed with the charming *insouciance* only to be seen in the amateur poet, painter, player, musician, &c. &c. And yet there is sometimes an earnest, thoughtful aspect about the youth that surprises one into the suspicion that all his levity is superficial, and hides his deeper and better nature, as stubble sometimes covers and conceals a mine of precious metal.

"Well!" at last spoke Mr. Fairfax, "it is now about twelve hours since we were emptied out of that atrocious old stage-coach, which, for a week past, has been beating us about in its interior from side to side, and from seat to ceiling, as if we were a lump of butter in an old woman's churn, and whose kindest turn of all to us was, when it turned over and shook us out down the precipice, and into the trough of the Wolf's Lick, as if we had been apples fed to the pigs! Oh, by the lost baronetcy of the house of Fairfax! my self-esteem will never recover the effects of it! Perdition seize the picturesque at this price! And ever since long before daybreak this morning have we been wandering about over these mountain-tops, with the earth below us hidden in mist, and only the highest peaks looming through the sea of vapour like islands in the ocean ; and *we* plunging wildly about in the fog, like Death on the pale horse riding the waves, and at the momentarily-recurring risk of riding over some hidden precipice of a thousand feet perpendicular. If this be your glorious mountain-scenery, to the demon with it! for I had as lief be on the open sea with the 'Ancient Mariner!'"

To this half-petulant, half-laughing philippic, Captain Clifton, while his glance still roved over the shrouded hemisphere, replied, with an indulgent smile—

"You cannot see the face of the country for the morning veil she chooses to wear. But wait till high noon, when the sun, her royal lover, in the meridian of his glory, shall raise that gauzy covering, and she, like a right royal bride, shall smile and blush in light and glory."

"By my soul, I could fancy the lady earth wore this veil to conceal fast-gathering tears, rather than smiles or blushes! *Anglice*, I think we shall have rain soon—though blistered be my tongue for saying it!—not about the rain, but about the veil! For, look you! fret as I may at this journey through the mist, yet this fine scenery, under a cloud as it literally *is*, gives me a feeling of breadth, grandeur! I expand, spread out over the vast area of its shrouded solitudes! Oh, it is only on the boundless sea or on the mountain-top, with a hemisphere below me, that I feel as if I had room enough to live in! And you give me a feeling of suffocation by drawing in this awful shrouded world to the simile of a lady's veiled face! But it is not to be wondered at. No, by the shade of Marc Antony, and all other great men who held the whole world light in the balance with a woman's evanescent smile or tear! everything is *apropos des femmes* with you now. Could the music of the spheres suddenly burst upon your astonished ears, as soon as you had recovered your senses, your highest note of admiration would be to compare that universal diapason of divine harmony to Lady Carolyn's silver laugh!"

"I do not recollect ever to have heard Lady Carolyn laugh."

"*Ten thousand pardons!* A Clifton of Clifton never laughs. But tell me, captain, whereabouts in the world—I mean, in the clouds—*are we?* And when shall we see this pure pearl of beauty and the rich casket that enshrines her; this stately lily of the mountains and the parterre where she blooms? When shall we behold Paradise and the Peri— Clifton and Lady Carolyn?"

Without replying to this mock-poetic strain, Captain Clifton remianed with his eyes still wandering from east to west, and back again over the rolling vapour. And Fairfax continued—

"I suspect, now, by your abstracted air and wandering eye, that you have lost your way in the clouds—not the first time such a thing has happened to a lover; nor would it be strange in a place like this, where the only landmarks are mountain-tops sticking out of the fog, with a day's journey between each!"

At this instant, a distant group of peaks broke suddenly through the mist like new isles thrown up by the sea, and glittered whitely in the sunlight against the deep blue horizon.

"See!" exclaimed Clifton, roused from his apathy by the sudden apparition. "Look, Fairfax! I will show you White Cliffs! Look straight before you to the western horizon—a little north of west. You see a crescent of seven peaks rising through the mist against the sky. That is White Cliffs."

"Looking white enough at this distance—quite like snow-capped mountains, in fact."

"Yes. They are of white quartz, and their peaks rising from the girdle of dark evergreens around their base and sides have quite a cooling effect in hot weather."

"Ah! just so. Now, how far off are those same blessed refrigerators?"

"About twenty-five miles in a bee-line. But the mountain-road is very circuitous, and makes the distance nearly forty. However, if we ride well, we shall be able to reach Clifton in time to surprise Mrs. Clifton at tea."

"Heaven be praised for that possibility!" ejaculated Fairfax, as they prepared to descend the mountain-side.

As they rode down, Captain Clifton, warming slightly from his cool reserve, said—

"I think, Fairfax, that you, poet and artist as you claim to be, will rather like Clifton. Tourists, who have visited our part of the country, think the scenery there very fine. It impresses me merely as being unique. There is something formal—but, to myself, not therefore unpleasing—in that crescent of seven peaks ; the tallest being in the centre and gradually declining thence to the lowest, which may be called the horns of the crescent, and point southward.   These peaks rise from a forest of—first elms and oaks around their base ; then pines farther up their sides ; and last of cedars, above which rise the pinnacle of white quartz. This crescent of mountains surrounds and shelters from the north winds the family mansion, which is situated in the woods at its foot. North of the peaks the country is wild and rugged, but partly covered with thick forest, and affording the best hunting-grounds in the world.   There you may course the hare ; track the deer ; or, if your tastes aspire to a fiercer conflict, hunt the wolf, the wild-cat, or the bear !"

" Or the rattlesnake, copper-head, or mocassin ! Thank you, I have no inclination for crusade against those mountaineers," laughed Fairfax.

" Perhaps you like angling ?   There is a trout-stream at the foot of the wooded lawn, in front of the house.   I must tell you about that, for it is the head waters of a fine river. From the western cliff there springs a torrent that, with many a leap, a fall, and rebound, tumbles tumultuously down the side of the mountain, and, falling into a channel at the foot of the lawn, flows calmly on until it meets a second fall, from whence it goes hurrying on, through forests, fields, and rocks, taking tribute from many a mountain-torrent, and many a meadow-stream, and widening as it goes, until it becomes a mighty river, rushing on to pour its floods into the majestic James.   After which, they both go on, breaking through range after range of mountains, and so conquer their passage to the sea—even as in the feudal days of the olden country, some mountain chieftain, gathering his vassals together, came rushing down from his Highland home, and, laying all the country under tribute in his course, hurried on to throw all his treasures at the feet of his sovereign, and go with him to the wars."

" Clifton !" said Fairfax more seriously than he had yet spoken, " all your illustrations, all your metaphors, all your thoughts, fancies, and imaginings, are, not ' of the earth, earthy,' but—worse, far worse—of the *world, worldly !*—of the world, its castes, customs, and conventions—its pomps, vanities, and falsities !   You speak of the grandest, the most imposing—oh! let me call it at once the most magnificent— area of mountain-scenery in the hemisphere, with all the earth, below and around, covered with a sea of vapour that rises and falls, rolling from horizon to horizon like the waves of the ocean, and you compare it to a veiled royal bride! You describe a mighty mountain-river, rending its passage through the everlasting rocks, overleaping, uprooting, bearing down and bearing on all obstacles to its resistless rush towards the sea, and you liken it to a chieftain going to pay tribute to a king! Ah, Clifton of Clifton! the beauty, the glory, and the majesty of the *earth* please you; but the 'pomp, pride, and circumstance' of the *world* inspire you! But when was it otherwise with a Clifton of Clifton? 'The spirit of intense worldliness has ever been their bane and curse—their sin and its punishment!'" he concluded, relapsing into his mock-tragic air.

"Ah! so you are familiar with the popular legend that you have just quoted," said Captain Clifton. "But," he added, with a sarcastic smile, "were Georgia here, I think she could refute the charge, and prove one Clifton, at least, has been guided by any spirit rather than that of intense worldliness."

"*Georgia?*"

"I beg her pardon! Mrs. Clifton of Clifton."

"Oh, your aunt! but by my soul, captain, that was a very irreverent way of introducing the old lady! Do young men in your patriarchal part of the country call old gentlewomen by their Christian names?"

"Old gentlewomen!" repeated Clifton slowly, with a musing smile, adding, "Georgia is about seventeen years of age, and the most beautiful woman in the world!"

"Whe-e-e-ew! I'm amazed! I'm confounded! I'm stunned! Then the present Mrs. Clifton is the *second* wife?"

"No, sir. Georgia is my uncle's fourth wife."

"Overwhelmed! annihilated!" exclaimed the young man. "The—the—old Blue Beard! the old Henry VIII.! Four wives! Are they all living?—if not, where does he bury his dead?"

"*Fairfax!*" exclaimed Captain Clifton in a tone and with a look that speedily recalled the young man to himself; then he added rather haughtily, "My Uncle Clifton is a simple, gentle-hearted old man, excessively fond of women; but mark you, sir! it is the affection of the patriarch, not of the pacha."

"Hang me if ever I saw any difference between Solomon the king, and Solimaun the caliph—Abraham the patriarch, and Aroun the pacha—in that respect," laughed the young man, until, stealing a furtive glance at the cold and haughty face of Clifton, he held out his hand, and suddenly exclaimed, "Pardon me, Clifton! or call me out! I can't help a jest, to save my soul! but I'll fight, or apologise, or render any other sort of satisfaction afterwards!"

Captain Clifton remembered that Francis Fairfax was his guest, going to spend a long midsummer furlough at his mother's house; and so he cleared his brow and answered, "Nonsense!"

"Now, tell me about Henry VIII.'s fourth queen. How long has she been married—I mean, the present Mrs. Clifton?"

"About two years. My uncle wedded her when she was fifteen—she is now seventeen, and, as I said, the most beautiful creature that you, or I, or anyone else ever did, or ever shall see, anywhere."

"*Allons*—stop there! False knight and recreant! whose colours do you wear while you uphold the peerless beauty of Georgia? What would Miss Clifton of Clifton say to your admiration?"

"Ridiculous, sir! Miss Clifton is herself very beautiful, but not the *most* beautiful. Miss Clifton has *other* and *rarer* distinctions, I am proud to say!"

"Oh, I understand—her family *name!* Nevertheless, be hanged if I don't believe you have been in love with Georgia!"

"Impossible, sir! The perfect beauty of the young girl struck me forcibly, as it strikes *all others*—nay, more, impressed my imagination deeply, perhaps. I confess to a *penchant* for female beauty; and, observe, it is the artist's taste, sir, not the sultan's. But in love with Georgia! Impossible, sir! She was a girl of humble parentage!"

"Ah! then you think it quite impossible that a gentleman born should be in love with a girl of humble parentage?"

"Preposterous, sir! utterly preposterous! Pray, let us hear no more about it!"

"Let your uncle—"

"My uncle married such an one, you would say. Old gentlemen living on their own estates will do such things; and the world charitably ascribes it to dotage, smiles, and forgives them. You will oblige me by changing the subject, Frank."

Fairfax fell into reverie, and Clifton dropped into thought, and they rode on for some time in silence and in joy, until—

"Floods and furies! Fire and flames! Lightning, and tempests, and sudden death!" exclaimed Fairfax, rearing and backing his horse with a terrible jerk, and throwing himself from the saddle, bathed in perspiration, and shaking with terror. "Look! Look there! There at your feet! Back! Back your horse, unless you wish to ride straight to the kingdom of heaven, or—to the other place! Oh, blessed Lord! I shall never survive the shock!"

Captain Clifton backed his horse, dismounted, and, following the index of Fairfax, approached the brink of the awful abyss, and looked down a perpendicular precipice of more than a thousand feet, with the remaining distance lost in shadows and dim vapours, while faintly to the ear came a low and hollow murmur, as of the roaring of many waters at a vast depth.

"This is the head of the Devil's Staircase! We have lost our way," said Captain Clifton.

"Devil's Staircase! I should think it was! Ugh! Oo-oo-oo-ooh! I shall never survive it! Where does it lead to? Tell me that! To the infernal regions, I suppose, of course. Ur-r-r-r-r!" exclaimed Fairfax, with his teeth chattering.

"We have indeed made a very narrow escape," said Captain Clifton, gazing thoughtfully down the horrible pit.

"Narrow escape! Ur-r-r-r-r!" exclaimed Frank, shaking, shuddering, and streaming with cold perspiration. "I tell you, when I was providentially led to look down, and saw the fog roll away from beneath my horse's feet, and reveal that ghastly—Ur-r-r-r-r! Ur-r-r-r-r! I believe I shall chatter my teeth to powder!"

"Come, come, Fairfax! this is really unmanly. Thank an ever-watchful Providence, that has preserved you from a sudden and horrible death, and calm yourself. Be a man!"

"Be a man! You might as well say to my shuddering horse there, 'Be a horse! This is unhorsely!' Ur-r-r-r-r! I tell you it has given me the tertian ague!"

"Why, Frank, really!"

"Look at my horse—look even at that dumb beast! Yes look at that gallant steed, who would charge upon a phalanx of fixed bayonets, and impale himself upon their points, if spurred to it—look at him! Positively frozen with terror!"

"Fairfax, you astonish me—certainly you are not really so much overcome."

"Overcome! My nerves are shattered to atoms, I tell you! Ur-r-r-r-r! It has given me the tertian ague, and the St. Vitus' dance—both together! Ur-r-r-r-r!"

"Now, who would have supposed you to be a— of such a nervous temperament? Come, let me assist you to mount, and then away."

"What! And at the end of the next hundred yards ride headlong over a precipice of fifteen hundred feet, and before night find sepulchre in the maws of fifty turkey-buzzards! I tell you there is neither a glorious death, an honourable burial, nor an immortal fame to be found in such a fate! Heavens and earth, no! For instance—'What ever became of that poor devil, Fairfax?' asks one. 'Oh, one day, crossing the mountains in a fog, with his head in a mist, he had the awkwardness to pitch himself headforemost down the Devil's Ladder, in the Alleghanies,' answers t'other. '*Poor creature!* He was always a miserable—but where was he buried?' 'He wa'n't buried—the crows eat him up,' &c. Oh! I know what my posthumous fame would be in such a case. Quite different from that of the future Major-General Francis Fairfax, who, fifty years hence, at a good old age, shall die in his downy bed, with the archbishop praying by him, and be buried with the highest honours of war, and have a national monument raised to his fame, emblazoning his immortal services to his grateful country, in receiving her honours and emoluments for more than half a century! Can't give up that glorious future for the sake of dashing myself to pieces this afternoon, Clifton. No!" said the young man, folding his arms, and striking an attitude *à la Napoleon*, "I have a destiny to fulfil, and shall not stir from this spot until the mist rises or falls."

"Mr. Fairfax, it is now drawing late in the afternoon. We shall have a storm before night; and a storm on the mountains, let me tell you, is a much more delightful thing to read about in Childe Harold, while stretched at your ease upon the settee in your shady piazza, than to take in *propria personæ* on the Alleghanies," said Captain Clifton quietly.

"Only warrant me from bringing up suddenly to the jumping-off place before I know it, and I'll make an attempt! Yea! let him only insure my body unharmed by fire or water, and I'll valiantly follow my leader through flood and flame!" replied Frank, recovering himself with a few more shudders, and preparing to mount.

"We have left the right road about two miles behind," said Captain Clifton, turning his horse's head and leading the way.

The fog below was condensing very fast. From the north-western horizon black clouds were rising behind masses of foaming white vapour. The air was still and oppressive, and from all around came a faint, low moaning sound, as if nature cowered and trembled before the coming of the terrible "storm-king." The fog was now rolling down and gathering into clouds below them—revealing the majestic features of the landscape, mountains, vales and forests, rocks, glens, and waterfalls, in wild and magnificent confusion—all wearing now a savage and gloomy aspect under the shadow of the coming storm. Captain Clifton's eye had been constantly on the alert in hope of discovering some mountain cabin, which might shelter them from the fury of the tempest, but as yet his search was unsuccessful—no human dwelling even of the humblest description was to be seen. At length the attention of the travellers was attracted by the faint tingling of a bell, then by the bleating of sheep, and then from the deep clouded glen at their right sprang up into their path a bell-wether, followed by two—five—ten —a whole flock of sheep, and driven by a girl on a pony; a little, coarse, sun-burned girl, in a boy's coarse straw hat and a homespun gown, riding on a little, rough-coated, wiry, mountain pony.

"A shepherdess, by all that is romantic!" exclaimed Fairfax, vaulting aside to let the sheep pass. Then springing to the side of the rough-coated pony, he doffed his hat to the rider and said, "My good girl, for the love of Providence will you tell us where we can find shelter from the storm?"

The child raised her fine eyes to the stranger's face with the look of a startled fawn, and dropped them again instantly. Fairfax repeated his question. The child stole another furtive glance at the fine gentleman in the very fine uniform, and then at her own coarse raiment, and blushed deeply. But before Fairfax could reiterate his request, she said quietly, "Grandfather's cabin is not far off, if you and the other gentleman will come with me."

"With great pleasure—and ten thousand thanks, my dear little girl. Be so good as to lead the way."

The flock of sheep had gone on before. The girl put her pony in motion, and the gentlemen followed—Mr. Fairfax addressing all his conversation to his little companion, and Captain Clifton riding on in silence and abstraction.

The sky was darkening very fast, and great single drops of rain occasionally falling. They quickened their pace, and, after riding briskly several hundred yards, came to the head of a glen, deep down in which was seen a small, lone cabin. At this instant the sheet-lightning glared from horizon to horizon, followed by a report as of exploded and falling rocks, and then the rain came down in a deluge. The darkness was so dense now as to hide their way. The girl jumped from her pony, and, giving him a little slap that sent him travelling down the path, went up to the head of Clifton's horse and said shyly—

"You can't see the way, sir, and you don't know the road—let me lead your horse."

"By no means, my good girl," replied Clifton, speaking in a tone of haughty astonishment.

Without reply, the child turned from him and went towards Fairfax. And at the same instant a thunderbolt was hurled from heaven with a terrific crash, riving the ground on which she had just stood. When the panic was over, the first thought of Captain Clifton was for the safety of that presumptuous child. A glare of lightning revealed her lying on the rock. He hastened to her side.

"My dear child, are you hurt?" he asked, dismounting and stooping to lift her.

"Oh, sir, I am so glad to hear you speak! I thought you were struck."

"Are you hurt?"

"Oh, no, sir, I was only thrown down," replied the child, lightly springing to her feet.

"Oh, yes! Exchange your mutual condolences and congratulations. But who the mischief cares whether I am hurt or not?" exclaimed Fairfax, stumbling along towards them; for he also had dismounted.

"You were entirely out of danger," replied Clifton.

"Out of danger! Who the deuce is out of danger within a hundred miles of these infernal mountains?"

The rain was still pouring down in floods, and, in the interval of the thunder, the roar of the swollen torrents was deafening. The question now was, whether to remain standing there exposed to all the fury of the storm, or to attempt the now dangerous descent into the glen.

"I could lead your horses down in safety, if you would let me, for I know every inch of the road so well," said the girl.

Another blinding glare of lightning, another terrific peal of thunder, and another deluge of rain, put a stop to all reply. At last the child repeated her offer, saying that she could lead the horses down very well, "one at a time." But, of course, that was not for a moment to be thought of by the young men; and her plan was rejected at once.

"Well, then, the only way will be to go down on foot, and leave your horses here to follow; for you will need your hands as well as your feet in groping down the slippery rock through the darkness," said the girl.

After a little more consultation, her last proposition was adopted, and they began the descent on foot.

After some twenty minutes' toil and struggle through darkness and deluge, thunder and lightning, they reached the lowly door of the cabin, pushed it hastily open, and hurried in.

It was very dark, and nothing was to be seen but the red glow of a few smouldering embers on the hearth. Towards these the girl went.

"And what do you think has become of your flock of sheep, my good girl?" inquired Frank kindly, remembering her interests while he stood there wringing the water out of his coat-skirts.

"Oh, the bell-wether has led them all into the pen long ago, sir. They are always safe when they are once in the glen," replied the child, as she lighted a candle.

The sudden glare of the light showed a rude apartment with an earth floor, log walls, and a fireplace of unhewn stone. On the right of the fireplace stood a poor bedstead, upon which lay a venerable, white-haired old man, covered with a faded counterpane; and near the bed sat an old chip-bottomed arm-chair. On the left of the fireplace were two rough plank shelves, the lower shelf adorned with a few pewter plates and mugs; the upper one filled with—books!—piles of old dingy, musty books; and near these shelves stood a spinning-wheel, with a broach of yarn on the spindle, and a basket of broaches under it. At the opposite end of the room, one corner was occupied by a little old oak table, and the other by a ladder leading up through a trapdoor into the loft over-head. A few rude stools were ranged along the walls; junks of smoked venison, ropes of onions, bunches of dried herbs, hanks of yarn, and the old man's old hat and coat, garnished the walls. All this was seen at a glance.

"Is your grandfather sick?" inquired Frank.

The girl turned her eyes wistfully towards the venerable sleeper, and did not reply

"Is your grandfather sick?" repeated Fairfax.

The child raised her eyes sorrowfully to the face of the young man, and remained silent.

"Is he so *very* sick?" earnestly reiterated Frank.

"He is not sick, sir," answered the girl in a low, sad voice.

"What is the matter with him, then?" thoughtlessly persisted Frank.

Without reply, the girl dropped her eyes, and, blushing deeply, turned away. Setting the candle down upon the table, she took a pail of water and went up the ladder and into the loft. After an absence of a few minutes, she returned, and said—

"If you will go up stairs now, you will find two suits of grandfather's and Carl's Sunday clothes. They are not fine, but they are clean and dry."

Our wet and jaded travellers thanked their young hostess, and prepared to accept her offer.

"And if," she added, "you would like to rest after so much fatigue, there is a bed."

They reached the loft, and found it a small, low place, with a little window, and a little, clean bed. On the bed lay the two suits of homespun, and two coarse towels; and on a stool near stood a pail of water and a tin basin.

"I do believe that little girl has given us her own sanctuary. What a dear little thing she is!—so full of courage, and shyness, too! If she were two or three years older, and a great deal prettier, I could fancy myself writing poetry about her," said Frank.

Clifton made no comment. He was engaged in divesting himself of his wet garments, and thinking about—Miss Clifton.

When they had refreshed themselves by washing and changing their dress, Frank threw himself upon the bed, stretched out his limbs luxuriously, and declared that the rustic's clothes were very loose and comfortable, and his own position truly delightful. Captain Clifton walked to the window, and looked out at the storm, which was now abating.

Frank was already sound asleep.

And while Clifton stood at the window, drawing comparisons between the meanness of the hut in which he found himself and the magnificence of the mountain-scenery around it, he heard, in that small, shell-like cabin—he could not help hearing—what follows. First a heave and plunge, as if the old man below stairs had started violently from his bed and fallen again; and then a fearful, shuddering voice exclaimed, "Kate! Kate! they're coming again! They're after me, Kate! They're on me! they're on me! Save me, Kate! save me, Kate! Save—"

"Grandfather, dear grandfather," said the soothing voice of the girl, "there is no one here but me. There, there, be quiet—be still; nothing shall hurt you here—nothing can, you know."

"Look! Look, Kate! look! They're not men now, but devils!" A violent plunge, struggles, exclamations of terror and despair which the low, soothing tones and gestures of the poor girl vainly essayed to tranquillise for some time, and then silence for a few minutes, which was again interrupted by "Snakes! snakes, Kate! Snakes! *Green* snakes! See! see how they dart! They fly! They're on me! They're on me! Help! help!" and the sound of the maniac laying about him furiously. Captain Clifton started up with the intention of going to the poor girl's assistance; but by the time he reached the head of the ladder, the voice of the child had again calmed the infuriated man.

All was quiet for a quarter of an hour, and then another violent start and throw that seemed to shake the little hut, and a horrible shriek of, "A dragon! a dragon, Kate! A green dragon belching flame!" Then a succession of violent shrieks and struggles, which aroused Frank, who, springing up in bed, exclaimed—

"What the deuce is the matter? Has the major got another fit of *mania-a-potu* on him?" Then, as all again was quiet, he rubbed his eyes and said, laughing, " I do believe I have been talking in my sleep! I dreamed we were in our mess, and the major was drunk again."

"A part of your dream was real. The old man below stairs has a fit of *mania-a-potu* upon him."

"What! and you staying here! I must go down and help the girl."

"You had better not as yet. She seems to have the power of soothing him. Your presence might, by exasperating him, do more harm than good."

At this moment another outbreak of fury from the madman caused Frank to spring to his feet, and, exclaiming, "I can't let that maniac tear my dear little hostess to pieces," rush to the head of the ladder.

"I tell you you had best not *intrude*. His mania seems perfectly harmless to the child."

But Frank was at the foot of the ladder, where, however, an impediment met him. The girl, who had just succeeded in again soothing the madman, came and stood before him, saying, "Pray do not come in, sir, just yet."

"But, my good girl, I must come in and remain to protect you," gently trying to pass her.

She stood her ground firmly; her *lips* said, " I am not in any danger. I beg you, sir, do not come in yet;" but her steady and rather threatening *glance* said, " Do not dare to look upon the old man in his degradation!"

Frank turned back, and went and perched himself at the top of the ladder to watch over the safety of the girl, and be ready in case of exigency.

He saw the old man lying, clutching the cover around him, while his terror-dilated eyes glared out like a wild beast's from its lair—all ready for another start and spring!

He saw the girl mix a mug of strong vinegar and water, and take it to him, and the old man grasp and quaff it with fiery thirst; three times she filled the mug, and three times he gulped its contents with voracity. Then she laid his aged head tenderly down, and went and saturated a cloth with vinegar, and placed it about his burning forehead and temples. Next she took a rustic fan of turkey feathers, and stood by him and fanned him until he fell into a sleep that every moment became deeper and deeper. Finally, she gently laid down the fan, sunk upon her knees by the bedside, and bowed her head upon her clasped hands in silent prayer. At last she arose, pressed a light kiss upon the furrowed brow of the sleeper, and silently went about her household work.

From a shed at the back of the house she brought wood and water, made up the fire, filled and hung on the tea-kettle, set an oven and oven-lid to heat, and again disappeared through the back door into the shed. In about fifteen minutes she returned with a tray of dough and a pan of venison steaks. She made her dough into a loaf and put it in the oven to bake, and prepared her venison steaks to lay upon the coals. She set her table with milk, and cream, and butter, brought in, doubtless, from a rude but cool spring-house, near at hand.

When all was done, she sat down to knit, seeming to wait the coming of another; for she often paused and listened with her head turned towards the door, and at length got up and drew from under the bed a trunk, whence she took an old, well-patched but clean suit of homespun clothes, with a shirt and a pair of socks, and hung them over a chair.

Soon after a step was heard without—the door was thrown open, and a thin, dark young man, dressed as a farm-labourer, entered. Throwing his coarse hat to the other end of the room, he approached the fire, when seeing the situation of the old man he stopped short, and, placing his arms akimbo, gazed on him, exclaiming, "Drunk again, by——!" and then turned with an interrogative look towards the girl.

A short wave of the hand, a quick, distressful nod, and the choking down of a sob, told him that it was so.

The young man let down his arms, and with a frown of mingled sorrow and anger approached and gazed upon the sleeper.

"Have you had much trouble with him, dear Kate?"